A Fairy Good Mystery

by

Linda Bullock Haver

The Reading Glass Books
1-888-420-3050
www.readingglassbooks.com
fulfillment@readingglassbooks.com

CONTENTS

This story is the result of a collaboration
between my grandchildren Lewis and
Neva Haver and myself.

Our brainstorming of ideas for a mystery
involving fairies grew with their ideas to
add other woodland creatures and themes
of friendship and working together.

Dedicated to all the children who have
stories to tell.

CHAPTER

1

Evie ran out of the door and yelled to her mom, "I'll be in my reading nook by the creek."

Mom looked up from her gardening and answered, "Enjoy the books, I can't wait to hear your ideas for the fairy garden you and Dad are planning."

Evie thought about how lucky she was to have a mom who was a librarian that worked part time at the town library. Evie would mention a subject to her mom and the next time her mom worked she would bring home books for Evie to read.

Today Evie was reading all about different types of fairies in stories from Great Britain. She wanted to get some ideas for a fairy garden her dad was helping her make under a tree in the backyard.

Evie's dad was a software engineer and usually worked from home, so he and Evie liked to do special projects together. Evie was excited that today was the first day of summer break from school. Evie didn't want to waste any time getting started on the fairy garden project.

When Evie got to her cozy outdoor reading and relaxing nook, she carefully laid her library books on a big rock that looked like a small table. A bigger rock that was curved in the back was her reading seat. A large oak tree shaded the area where the sounds of the creek made a relaxing place to sit. Her reading nook had been one of the projects Evie and her dad had worked on two summers ago when Evie finished first grade.

Evie finished two chapters of her first book and decided to take a break. When she stood up to stretch her legs, she noticed something shiny laying in the grass on the edge of the creek. It looked like a sparkling stone catching the sunlight.

"This will be the perfect addition to my special nature collection," thought Evie. When Evie leaned over to pick it up, she noticed something that looked like glittery letters on the front of the stone. She could read "H-E", but the next few letters were very blurry.

"Who could have left this stone here?" thought Evie.

Evie decided she should talk to Randy to see if he had left the stone by the creek bank.

Randy was Evie's friend that lived in the next house down the creek. He was a year younger than Evie and they had been besties their whole lives.

If Randy hadn't put the stone there for her to find, there was a mystery to solve. Luckily Evie and Randy loved mysteries.

CHAPTER

2

When Evie got back to her house her grandparents were there for a surprise picnic celebrating the end of school and beginning of summer. They were anxious to hear everything about Evie's last days of third grade. Evie was so busy telling stories about her fun school adventures she forgot all about the glittery stone she had found earlier.

Early the next morning Evie remembered finding the stone and asked her mom if she could go over to Randy's house. Mom reminded Evie that Randy was visiting his aunt and uncle and wouldn't be home until the next day.

Evie didn't want to tell Mom about the special stone just yet because she wanted the fun of solving the mystery with Randy.

After helping straighten up the house, Evie grabbed her library books and headed back to her reading nook.

When she put her books on the big rock table, she noticed another shiny stone lying on the ground. She picked it up and saw glittery letters that looked like P-L-E, then more blurry letters.

"Another clue to the mystery!" said Evie excitedly. "Randy couldn't have left this stone here because he is away. Someone is trying to leave me a message and I don't know what it means. I can't wait to see Randy tomorrow. He is very good at solving mysteries."

Evie tried very hard to calm down and spend some time reading her books, but all she could think about was the two messages on the stones- H-E and P-L-E. What was someone trying to tell her? Did the message mean someone needs her to do something? The more she thought about the problem, the more confused she got.

Chapter

3

The next morning Evie peeked out of her bedroom window and noticed Randy's family car in his driveway. She hurried to get dressed then ran to Randy's house. She couldn't wait to tell him about the clues that she found by the creek. She was sure there was a mystery to solve.

Randy's mom opened the door and told Evie that Randy was in his room unpacking. Evie ran upstairs to his room.

Evie was very patient while Randy emptied his suitcase. She even let him tell her all about everything he did and saw on his vacation. But after a few more minutes she couldn't wait one more second.

"I have a mystery for us to solve!" Evie shouted.

Randy looked at Evie with a confused look. "What are you talking about?" he asked.

Evie explained all about the mysterious stones with blurry messages she had found by the creek.

Randy's eyes lit up with excitement. "We need to solve this mystery, let's get started."

4

Randy and Evie hurried downstairs to tell his mom they were going to play by the creek. Then they raced over to Evie's reading nook.

Evie grabbed the two stones she found earlier from under a bush. She had hidden them there so they would be safe. Randy held the stones in his hand and carefully inspected the letters on the rocks.

"I think this one with the letters H-E might say H-E-L-P. You can tell there are two more letters after the H-E, but I can't read them."

Randy and Evie both looked at the second stone for more clues. Just then, out of the corner of his eye Randy spotted another sparkling stone lying on the ground near the creek. He bent down, picked it up, and saw the letters H-U-R.

"I think I found another clue," Randy shouted to Evie. "Someone is trying to tell us something with these three clues. Let's sit down and try to decide what to do next."

Evie and Randy both agreed that they needed to look for more clues. They searched all along the creek and near the reading nook. They found many other rocks and stones but none of them had letters written on them. They were about ready to give up and ask their parents for help when Randy heard a very quiet voice coming from the creek bank.

Randy concentrated and listened very carefully with a determined look on his face. He wasn't quite sure, but it sounded like the voice said, "Please hurry, we need help."

CHAPTER

5

Randy called to Evie, "Come quickly, I think I heard a quiet voice near the creek asking for our help. It is very strange because I don't see anyone else around here. Do you think it was my imagination?"

Evie ran over to Randy, stood very still, and listened. "I think I hear it too, but the bullfrogs, crickets and birds are so loud I can't really be sure."

Then like magic, the frogs stopped croaking, the crickets stopped chirping, and the birds stopped singing. The creek was silent. Then Randy and Evie both clearly heard, "Please hurry, we need help!"

"We must figure out where the tiny voice is coming from. It probably has something to do with the messages we found on the rocks," Evie said excitedly.

Randy leaned down by the side of the creek. "I think I see something. Look down there," he pointed to the ground. "Can you see what is making the sounds?"

Evie got down on her hands and knees and looked through the tall grass growing at the edge of the creek. She noticed a dragonfly perched on a blade of grass. It looked like there was something on the dragonfly's back. Evie took a closer look and blinked her eyes. "I can't believe my eyes Randy. You'll never believe what I see!"

CHAPTER

6

Randy bent down to take a closer look at what Evie was so excited about. He rubbed both of his eyes because he couldn't believe what he saw. He took a closer look and realized a tiny fairy was sitting on the back of a dragonfly.

The fairy spoke up again. "Please we need your help! We left you those stones to get your attention. Our home is being destroyed by the creek and we don't know what to do to stop the rising water. Our fairyland community has lived here for many years and have welcomed many other creatures to join our home in the creek bank. Now we are all in danger."

Another shaky voice in the grass called out, "Please help us save our home. It is all my fault. I caused all these problems, and I don't know what to do to fix everything."

Randy and Evie looked down to see where the voice was coming from. They were both shocked to see a tiny gnome shaking and crying.

The gnome said his name was Gary. He talked so fast. Randy and Evie had a hard time hearing what Gary was saying. They did hear enough to understand that the fairyland was in danger because of water flooding in from the creek.

Evie shouted, "I will run and get my mom and dad. They will know what to do!"

The fairy and gnome both yelled, "NO! Wait, we can't get any adults involved."

CHAPTER

7

Evie was so surprised she suddenly stopped and looked at Randy. "What should we do?" Evie asked. "I know our parents will be able to help."

Randy answered, "Let's give them a chance to explain why they don't want us to get our parents. They must have a good reason."

The fairy spoke up. "Our fairy code is very important to us, and we are forbidden to spend time with grown-ups. Adults can't see or hear magical woodland creatures like us. All humans are born with the ability to see and hear us, but they lose that ability when they turn 10 years old. We try not to be seen or heard by children after they learn to talk because the adults would not understand when their children told stories about seeing and talking with woodland creatures.

"Evie," the fairy continued, "I have known you since you were a little baby. Your parents would bring you to the creek for a picnic and put you on a blanket to play. I would fly down and sit with you and make you laugh. Your parents never knew why sometimes you would just laugh out loud. They were always very excited that you were having a good time, but they never knew the whole story."

"I have had dreams about talking to fairies, dragonflies, butterflies, and gnomes," said Evie. "I thought it was just my imagination. I never, ever would have believed that really could have happened. Now I know they were really memories."

The fairy smiled. "When you were a toddler you loved to pick wild violets, so I decided my name would be Violet. We have been watching over you your whole life. We have enjoyed seeing you grow up. Sometimes we hear you read out loud and use funny voices when you are in your reading nook. We love to hear the stories, so we gather in the weeds to listen. It has been so exciting to watch you grow."

"We decided to show ourselves to you now Evie because we know we can trust you. Do you think you can help us?"

Evie and Randy smiled, and both happily nodded yes.

CHAPTER

8

"Before we get started, let me tell you everything about the history of Fairyland so you can decide how to help us fix our big problem," explained Violet.

"My four fairy friends and I came to this creek many years ago. We were searching for a safe, comfortable place to build our homeland. First, we made friends with all the dragonflies, ants, beetles, and butterflies. Our insect friends told us they would help us build a safe place where we could all live together. It sounded like a great idea, so we got started."

"The ants did most of the digging and made a main tunnel into the creek bank. We all helped make the tunnels wider and built rooms off the main tunnel. We had so much fun spending time together in our safe, cozy home."

"Everything seemed great at the beginning, but then we had a big storm with heavy rain, and the creek water got so high it ruined our home. We moved out and all lived under leaves of the big oak tree until we decided what to do next."

"Luckily a few days later a group of six tiny, strong gnomes happened to be traveling along the creek looking for a new place to live. We invited them to join our group."

CHAPTER

9

"Just a minute," said Randy. "Don't fairies and gnomes have special powers? Why can't you just fix the problem with your magic?"

"It's true we can do some magic," replied Violet. "When we were trying to get you to hear us calling to you, I used my magic and all the creatures of the creek got quiet, so you could hear us talking. Fairy powers can work on living things, but we have no magical powers over other objects."

While Violet was talking, she was joined by a different tiny gnome. She introduced the gnome named Trusty. Violet explained that the gnomes were given new names when they joined Fairyland. The gnomes' new names were earned by their actions toward the other woodland creatures.

Evie and Randy were both anxious to hear the rest of the history of Fairyland. So, Trusty gave Violet a break from talking and continued the story.

"We gnomes were so happy to be invited to be part of the Fairyland community. We all worked very hard to rebuild the creek bank home. Gnomes are strong and we were able to help the ants build better tunnels. We all worked together to make Fairyland a safe place to live. We even got a family of beavers to show us how to make a dam around our entire structure. We were happy for many years."

"When did things change?" asked Evie. "What happened to start the problem?"

"Well,'" said Trusty, "It all started when Gary, the gnome you met earlier, became jealous of the rest of the gnomes. Five of the gnomes, Busy, Friendly, Energetic, Truthful and I, had already earned our new names by showing how we could help our ever-growing community. But Gary always complained about everything and never did his fair share of the work. He never earned a new name and that made him angry. We tried to help him find something he enjoyed doing so he could be helpful, but he never even wanted to try."

"About a week ago, Gary left Fairyland. He tried

living in the woods by himself. While he was alone, he got madder and madder. He decided to secretly create a problem in Fairyland, then fix the problem all by himself so everyone would think he was a hero and give him a great new name.”

CHAPTER

10

Evie and Randy sat on the ground listening carefully to every word Trusty said. "What happened next?" asked Randy.

Trusty got back to the story. "Gary snuck back to Fairyland during the night and poked many giant holes in the dam surrounding our home. Then he joined the rest of us inside and just pretended nothing had happened."

"A few days later, it rained all night. In the morning water started leaking into Fairyland. Gary worked very hard to fix the leaks, but they kept getting bigger and bigger. Gary never paid attention when the beavers were teaching the gnomes how to build the dam, so he didn't know what to do. The holes got so big the whole dam collapsed. Luckily everyone got out safely before the walls came down."

"Wow," said Evie. "I guess you really do need help. Can the beavers help you again?"

Violet answered this time. "No, the beavers have all moved a long way down the creek to a big pond."

"I'm sure we can help," said Randy. "It's getting late, so we need to go home. But we will be back in the morning with some tools."

"Don't forget to wear your boots," yelled Violet. "It is very wet and muddy by our home."

CHAPTER

11

The next morning Randy met Evie by the creek, ready to go. "I brought some garden tools and small pails we can use to help rebuild Fairyland." Randy showed all the tools to Evie. "I told my dad we wanted to clean up around the reading nook and get rid of all the weeds. I always help Dad in the garden so he knows I can use the tools safely."

Evie and Randy both looked up when they heard a fluttering sound coming quickly toward them. They saw Violet and four other tiny fairies riding on dragonflies and butterflies. All the dragonflies and butterflies landed on the grass, then the fairies flitted over to where Evie and Randy were standing.

"Good morning, Evie and Randy," said Violet. "These

are my fairy friends that I told you all about yesterday. Their names are Daisy, Rose, Buttercup, and Petunia. We are here to lead you to Fairyland. Thank you so much for coming to help us. As we told you before, fairies are not supposed to reveal themselves to children who are old enough to talk, so this seems very strange to us. But, because of our emergency we felt it was our only choice."

Evie and Randy told the fairies not to worry because they would never tell anyone about Fairyland.

"Let's hurry," urged Daisy. "Our friends are waiting for us by the creek."

CHAPTER

12

Dragonflies and butterflies can be very shy around humans, so they flew off by themselves. Evie and Randy followed the fairies who were flitting along just above the grass.

When Evie looked down very carefully, she noticed a group of gnomes standing near some ants and beetles. "I think we are close," Evie whispered to Randy. "I still can't believe this is happening."

"Me either," Randy added. "When I came home from my vacation, I would never have believed I would be meeting and talking with all these creatures."

When they got a little closer, Trusty ran out of a bush to welcome them. He showed them the door to Fairyland.

It looked like big clumps of mud stuck to the side of the creek. Neither Randy nor Evie would have guessed that inside was the cozy home of all these friends.

Trusty said, "You can see where we made some patches with mud. It helped slow down the water but did not fix the problem. The mud will wash away in the next big rain."

Busy, Friendly, Energetic, Gary, and Truthful joined the others and asked what they could do to help. The ants and beetles cannot be heard by humans, so they whispered a message to the gnomes. They said to tell Evie and Randy that they wanted to help too.

Randy shared important information that he had learned last night. He had done a lot of reading and had come up with a few ideas that might work to save Fairyland.

Energetic got so excited he shouted, "Let the work begin."

Everyone agreed and asked Randy where to start.

CHAPTER

13

Randy asked all the gnomes to find sturdy sticks. Gary was the first one to take off running. Gary was really trying hard to be helpful to try to make up for all his mistakes.

Evie, the fairies, ants, and beetles started peeling the mud off the opening to Fairyland. When the mud was gone Evie peeked in the door and saw the tunnels and rooms where the friends lived.

"Wow, I can see you all worked very hard to create this amazing place to live," Evie said. "I sure hope Randy's ideas work and we can fix all the problems in your home."

Randy joined Evie, who was standing in the shallow creek so she could reach the mud opening. "I'm sure glad we wore our boots, this water is chilly," Evie told Randy. "It's a good thing the water in not deeper or we would be soaked."

Randy saw all the gnomes coming back to the creek. Each one was carrying a stack of sticks.

Randy called out to the gnomes, "Put the sticks in a big pile by the creek. Great job, I think that will be enough wood to build what I have in mind. Hopefully it will work."

CHAPTER

14

Everyone was very excited to hear Randy's clever idea about how to use the sticks. It got very quiet as all the friends listened patiently to everything Randy said.

Randy started to explain. "I read in one of my books that some people in Africa build special huts for their homes. The huts they make are super strong and hold up to heavy rain. I thought we could copy their way of building. We can make the outside wall where the door is now a super strong structure that the creek and rainwater can't get through."

"Wait," Gary interrupted. "How will we get in and out of our home?"

Randy smiled and said, "Good question. Don't worry,

Gary. I think you will like my plans for the new doors. But first, let's get started on the brand-new outside wall."

"First, Evie and I will weave the sticks into a large wooden wall. Then we will use the plastic twine I brought in my tool kit to tie the sticks together. That will be the base for the new wall. One time my dad told me that there is clay under the dirt near the creek. The gnomes, ants, and beetles can go dig up some clay while we are working on the wooden wall."

Rose asked, "What can the fairies do? We want to help too."

"I have an idea," Evie said after she noticed a shallow puddle near the creek. I will add more water to that puddle, then you fairies can put the sticks in the puddle to soak. The water will soften the sticks and make it easier to weave them together. When the sticks are ready, you can bring them to Randy and me."

"Great," said Rose. "Let's get started."

15

Randy and Evie worked very carefully to weave all the sticks together to make a wall. Then they tied the twine around the cross sticks to make it sturdier. They were just finishing when the gnomes, beetles, and ants came back carrying piles of wet clay on jar lids.

"We hope you don't mind," said Trusty, "but we took some of the lids off the jars in your recycling bin to use as trays to carry the clay."

"Of course we don't mind," laughed Evie. "I think that is a very smart way to recycle jar lids. When your new home is done, Randy and I can find some other recycled things that might be helpful for your community."

"Next we need to place the stick wall over the hole and fill the gaps with the clay," Randy told his friends. Evie, the fairies, and Friendly can hold the wall in place. The other gnomes, the ants, the beetles, and I can put in the clay. Then while that is drying, we can all think about where we should make the new doors to Fairyland."

Everyone worked very hard and soon the wall was in place in the bank of the creek. Gary worked extra hard to make sure the wall was level and airtight. The first step was done.

CHAPTER

16

"What is the plan for our new doors?" Gary asked Randy. Gary was so happy to see their home being rebuilt he didn't want to waste even one minute.

"I think we should make three separate slanted tunnels from your home up the surface of the soil," Randy answered. "That will make it much easier to escape if there is a problem. Everyone can look around near the creek and find a safe place for a door. We need three safe places to enter and exit."

Buttercup was the first one to find a good place for a door. "Look here under this bush. The bush will hide the door so no one else can see it and there is enough room for everyone from Fairyland to get in and out. We can even add some more camouflage around the door so no one would ever think it was there."

Randy and Evie ran over to the bushes near Buttercup to check it out.

"This will be a great place for an entrance," Evie agreed. "No one would ever guess a door was hiding under the bush."

Then several ants hurried over to a rock in Evie's reading nook. Trusty shouted, "I think the ants have found another good place for a door. Look by the reading nook. There is a gap where the two rocks meet that could be used for door number two."

After a few more minutes, Evie found a large root on the oak tree that had an open space under one part of it. "This is a perfect place," she shared, "and well hidden."

Randy smiled, "We're ready to get started."

Chapter

17

The ants and beetles got started on the tunnel under the bush. The ground was very hard, and the work was slow. Randy thought of a good idea that just might help to make the digging get easier. He dipped a bucket in the muddy creek, then poured the water over the ground to make it softer. Evie helped him and soon all three digging spots had softer soil. The ants and beetles got back to work.

Gary also had an idea, but he wanted to keep it a secret until he could see if it would work. He left the creek and hurried into the thick forest. Everyone was so busy they did not notice him leave.

Evie was taking a rest when she saw Gary coming

out of the forest with three friends. She yelled to Gary, "Where have you been?"

Gary was out of breath but was able to introduce his friends. "These are moles that I met when I left Fairyland and spent time in the forest. They agreed to help us dig the tunnels. Moles are champion tunnel makers and will have the tunnels done in no time."

Everyone cheered as the moles continued the digging that the ants and beetles had started. Soon the three tunnels into Fairyland were done.

After a short rest, and a thank you from everyone, the moles said good-bye and went back to their homes in the forest.

Randy checked to make sure the three doors to Fairyland were well camouflaged. "No one will ever notice these doors. Evie and I will be the only humans to know they are here."

CHAPTER

18

After the moles left, the rest of the friends finished up the outside work. Randy and Evie gathered pails of mud to pack over the clay and stick wall. The fairy, gnome, ant, and beetle friends all worked together to push the mud in the open places to camouflage the wall that they had worked so hard to build.

Randy explained that a very heavy rain might wash away some of the mud, but the clay and stick wall would stay strong even in very heavy rain. Gary volunteered to be the one in charge of checking the mud on the wall after every rainstorm.

When the work was done, Violet made a very important announcement. "First, I want to say thank you to everyone who came together to fix Fairyland. To Evie and Randy, your ideas and help saved our community, and we are forever grateful. To every special member of our community, we all proved that when we work together, we can accomplish anything."

"Now Trusty and I have a very special surprise," Violet continued. "Gary, even though you made a big mistake that hurt Fairyland, you worked very hard to correct that mistake. We know that you learned an important lesson and will now try your best to make the right choices. So Trusty and I would like to officially give you a new Fairyland name. You earned the name, Helpful."

Everyone there clapped and cheered, "Hurrah for Helpful!"

Gary's face blushed bright red as he said, "Thank you all so much for the new name. It really means a lot to me. But I would just like to keep the name Gary. As Gary I have learned many important lessons and now my name is special to me."

All the friends laughed and agreed. Gary is a special name for a good friend.

Evie and Randy decided to go home because they were too big to be helpful with fixing the rooms inside the new Fairyland. They both promised to come back in the morning to bring recycled items to be used to make all the new rooms more comfortable.

The woodland creatures waved good-bye and got busy working on the inside of their home.

CHAPTER

19

The next morning after breakfast, Randy and Evie met at the edge of Evie's backyard. They both carried small bags of items they had collected around their houses. They were so excited to share the everything with the Fairyland community.

As they started walking toward the muddy creek, the dragonflies and butterflies flew by to say hello. When they got closer to the creek, Gary ran over to greet them.

"Fairyland looks amazing," Gary shouted with joy. "I wish you could see the inside. We finished all the rooms, and they are dry and cozy."

"Great," said Randy. "Evie and I brought some things that might help your home feel even better."

"Wait one minute," Gary said as he slipped through the door under the bush. When Gary came back, all his friends from Fairyland were with him. "I wanted everyone to see what you brought for us, so we can all thank you."

Evie shared her things first. She showed them buttons of all sizes and colorful bottle caps. "I think you will be able to use some of these for dishes. These scraps of fabric and spools of thread can be used to make many useful things. I also found dollhouse furniture in our basement that should be just the right size."

Randy was next. "I found some old pieces of games that I thought would be helpful for you. There are some checkers, dice, little cars, and plastic-colored discs. I know you can think of some good ways to use them. I also brought strips of foam that could be used to make nice soft beds."

The fairies and gnomes all did happy dances as they looked over all the items. "Thank you! Thank You!" they all chanted to Evie and Randy.

Then Violet slowly stepped forward with a sad look on her face. "You both have done so much for us, and we never could have solved our big problem without you. We all appreciate your help, and you will always be our friends, but we will no longer be able to communicate with you or be seen by you. Remember we told you fairies are supposed to stay away from children that are old enough to talk. We trust you but can no longer break this rule because our emergency is over."

Randy spoke first. "We are very sad about not seeing everyone again, but we understand the rules We will never forget our amazing adventure with all of you."

"From now on I will be sure to spend more time reading out loud in my reading nook," added Evie. "If you ever need our help again, just send us a message."

Evie and Randy gave one last wave to their friends and turned to walk home. Even though they were both sad, they were glad they were able to solve the mystery that led to an adventure they would never forget.

CHAPTER
20

The next day Evie's dad offered to take Evie and Randy to the craft and garden stores to buy everything they needed to make a special fairy garden in the backyard. Evie had forgotten about the fairy garden project because she was so busy with Fairyland. Now she was excited to get started on a new project.

When they got to the store, Dad showed them the aisle that had all the supplies for a fairy garden. Dad saw a friend of his at the end of the aisle, so he left Randy and Evie to pick out items while he talked with his friend.

They picked out a couple of fairy houses, a bridge, trees, and a pretend lake. Then Evie found a fairy figurine that looked just like Violet. She said, "We have to get this one Randy." Randy smiled and agreed.

"Look Evie," Randy pointed out tiny gnome figurines. "I will look for ones that look like our friends."

Evie searched all the fairy figurines and found four more that looked like Rose, Petunia, Daisy, and Buttercup. Randy was able to find six figurines that reminded him of each of the gnomes.

They even found butterflies and dragonflies on stakes that would look great in the garden. Evie's dad joined them just as they were carefully putting the fairy and gnome figurines in the shopping cart.

Dad had a puzzled look on his face when he looked in the shopping cart. "I don't think gnomes live in fairy gardens, are you sure these are what you want?"

"Yes," answered Evie and Randy with big grins on their faces. "These are exactly what we want."

"Okay," said Dad. "If you are sure."

Randy whispered in Evie's ear. She smiled and asked her dad, "Can we also get some lifelike plastic insects for our fairy garden?"

"Why not," Dad laughed. "It is an imaginary garden so you can do whatever you want."

Evie and Randy both giggled to themselves when dad said "imaginary". They knew when they were done, this would be the second-best fairyland they had ever seen.

CHAPTER
21

The next morning Evie's dad, Evie and Randy got all the supplies together and started making a fairy garden under the big tree by the deck.

Dad cleaned out a large space under the tree and used stones that Evie and Randy collected to make a border around the space.

Dad had to go in the house to take a work call. While he was gone Evie and Randy worked together and drew a picture that showed where they wanted everything to go in the fairy garden. They were so busy working they didn't notice a rustling noise in the bushes by the woods. If they had looked up at just the right moment, they might have noticed a dragonfly with a fairy on its back flying into those bushes.

"That was a close one," whispered Rose to her friends hiding in the bushes. "For a second, I thought they saw me."

Trusty spoke up, "I am glad we get to see Evie and Randy making their own fairy garden. Tonight, when it is dark, and all the humans are sleeping we can go check out all their hard work. I'm glad that we get to see them from a distance since we can't talk with them anymore." Violet nodded and added, "I can't wait until the next time Evie reads a story out loud in her reading nook." Everyone gave a silent cheer to agree with Violet.

Evie and Randy finished their picture. They had no idea that their new friends were so close by.

When Dad came back, Evie and Randy showed him the picture they made.

Dad looked at the picture and smiled, "You both have such great imaginations. I don't know how you came up with the idea of having camouflaged openings that lead to underground tunnels. Also, the idea of fairies riding dragonflies and butterflies is so clever. I never would have thought of having so many creatures living together. This certainly will be the best fairy garden ever."

Evie and Randy both smiled and thanked Dad.

When the fairy garden was done Evie asked Randy a question. "Do you think we will ever see our woodland friends again?"

Randy answered, "Who knows what will happen in the future? But I do know that every time I see a dragonfly or a butterfly I will look closely to see if it is carrying someone on its back."

Discussion Questions

1. Why do you think Evie and Randy enjoyed solving mysteries?

2. Why do you think the fairies left secret messages on the stones before they talked to Evie and Randy?

3. Why did the fairy and gnome stop Evie and Randy from getting their parents involved?

4. Why do you think the fairies trust Evie enough to ask for her help?

5. How would you describe Gary the gnome at the beginning of the story?

6. If fairies can flit along above the ground, why do you think they sometimes ride dragonflies and

butterflies?

7. What evidence in the story shows Evie and Randy
   like to read?

8. Why was it important to camouflage the new doors
   to Fairyland?

9. What are some ways the woodland friends could
   use the recycled things Evie and Randy gave them?

10. Why did Evie say that now she would be reading
    aloud more often in her reading nook?

11. How did Gary the gnome change at the end of the
    story?

12. Why did Evie and Randy grin when dad said gnomes
    do not live in fairy gardens?